MOUSE'S FIRST SNOW

LAUREN THOMPSON

ILLUSTRATED BY BUKET ERDOGAN

SCHOLASTIC INC.
New York Toronto London Auckland
Sydney Mexico City New Delhi Hong Kong

One bright, white winter day,
Mouse and Poppa went
out to play!

"Let's go sledding!" said Poppa.
Whoosh, swoosh!

Poppa slid down the hill.

I can do that too! thought Mouse.

Pliff, Ploof!

Mouse slid down the hill too.

"Good for you!"
said Poppa.

"Let's go skating!" said Poppa.

Zzzipity, zzzip!

Poppa glided across the ice.

I can do that too! thought Mouse.

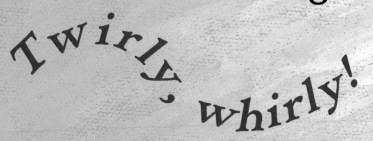

Twirly, whirly!

Mouse glided across the ice too.

"Hooray!" said Poppa.

"Let's make snow angels!"
said Poppa.

Swish, wish!

Poppa made angel wings
in the snow.

I can do that too! thought Mouse.

Flap, flop!

Mouse made angel wings
in the snow too.

"Wonderful!"
said Poppa.

"Let's make a snow house!"
said Poppa.

Push, pile!

Poppa built a grand snow house.

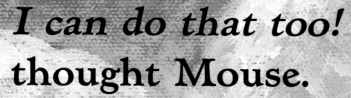

I can do that too!
thought Mouse.

Pitty-pat!

Mouse built a
grand snow house too.

"Good work!" said Poppa.

"Let's make a surprise!"
said Poppa.

Tumble, rumble!

Poppa rolled a round snowball.

I can do that too!
thought Mouse.

Roly, poly!

Mouse rolled a
round snowball too.

"Just right!" said Poppa.

Then,

tipsy-turvy, climb on top . . .

. . . pick, poke, a snowy grin . . .

"Look!" said Poppa.
"A frosty little snow mouse
just like you!"

"Happy winter, Mouse!"

To Robert and Owen—L. T.

To the peacefulness that snow brings, and to a peaceful world—B. E.

ISBN 978-0-545-32235-5

12 11 10 9 8 7 6 5 4 3   11 12 13 14 15/0

Printed in the U.S.A.   40

First Scholastic printing, December 2010

Book design by Einav Aviram